Mindfulness with Aloha Breath

KINDNESS

HARMONY

GENTLENESS

HUMILITY

PATIENCE

by Thao "Kale'a" Le

illustrated by Storm Aolani Kano

© 2020 Thao Le

ISBN 978-1-948011-37-2

Library of Congress Control Number: 2020908811

Legacy Isle Publishing
1000 Bishop St., Ste. 806
Honolulu, HI 96813
www.legacyislepublishing.net
info@legacyislepublishing.net

Printed in Korea

for keiki in Hawaiʻi and everywhere

"Who's to blame?
Who's to blame for my gain in pain?!"
exclaimed Stomach.
'ōpū

"It's you, Mouth! You're to blame!"
waha

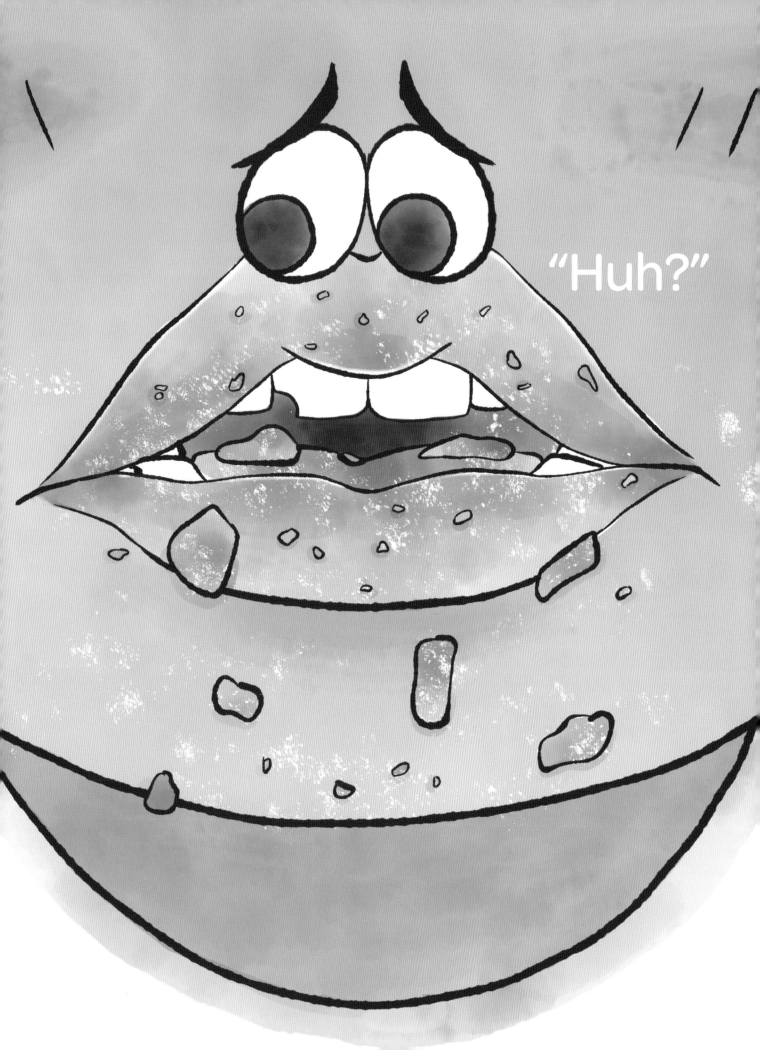

waha
"In me, Mouth, the malasadas land.
I taste, I chew, that's what I do.
But they are here
because of Hands."
lima

lima
"Hey, Hands,
you're to blame!"

"We grab, we hold, that's what we do.
We follow the lead, guided by Feet."
wāwae

wāwae
"It's you, Feet,
you're to blame!"

"We stand, we walk, we run,
that's what we do.
But who's our guide,
other than Eyes!"
maka

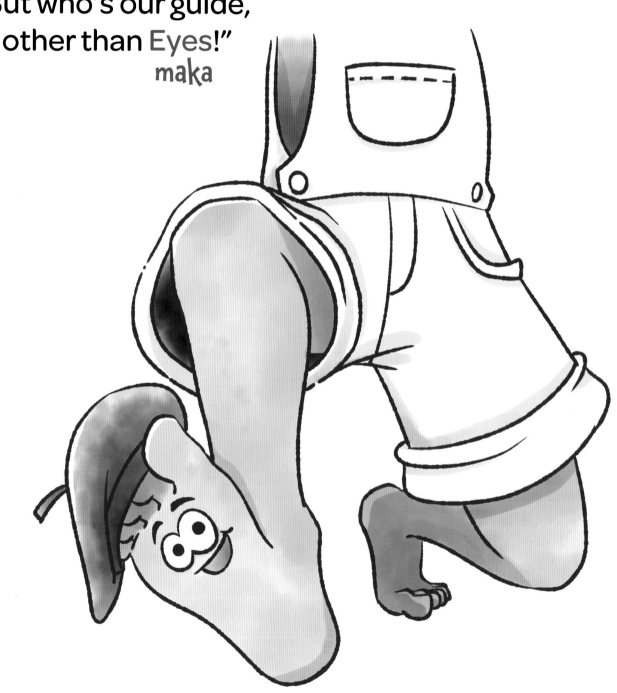

"It's you, Eyes, you're to blame!"
maka

"We see,

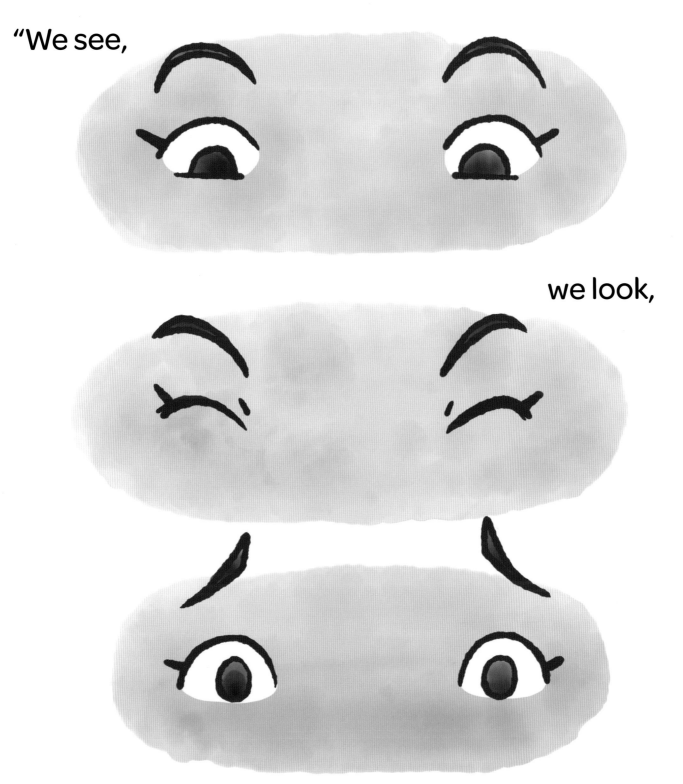

we look,

we can get spooked.

That's what we do."

"But who hears and directs us here?

pepeiao

It's you, Ears, you're to blame!"

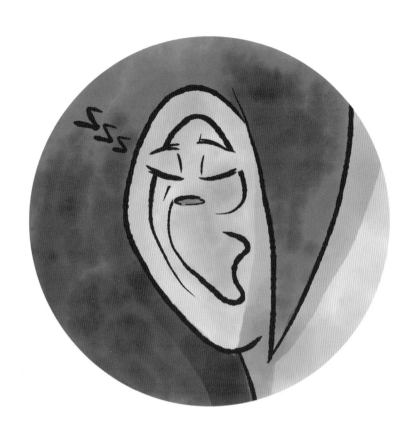

"We hear, we listen, that's what we do."

"But it's Nose, our neighbor,
who sniffs out the odors it prefers and favors."

"It's you, Nose,
you're to blame!"

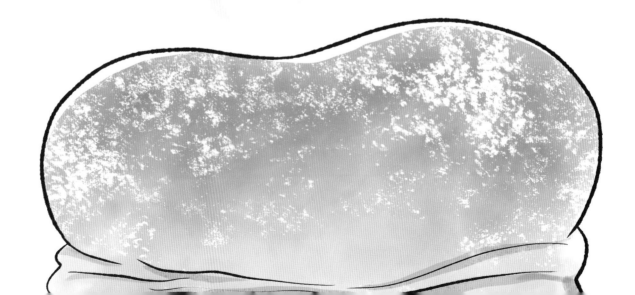

"Sniff, sniff,

I can tell the smell.

That's what I do."

"We contract, we expand, sharing all the air we can.
But below our frame there is a delicate one,
hidden, who could be the one to blame!"

"I beat, I supply the nutrients of life,"
says tender Heart.
puʻuwai

"But I say it's the one upstairs
who commands most affairs."

na'auao
"It's you, Brain, commander in charge,
with your electrical discharge,
you're the one who tells me what to do!"

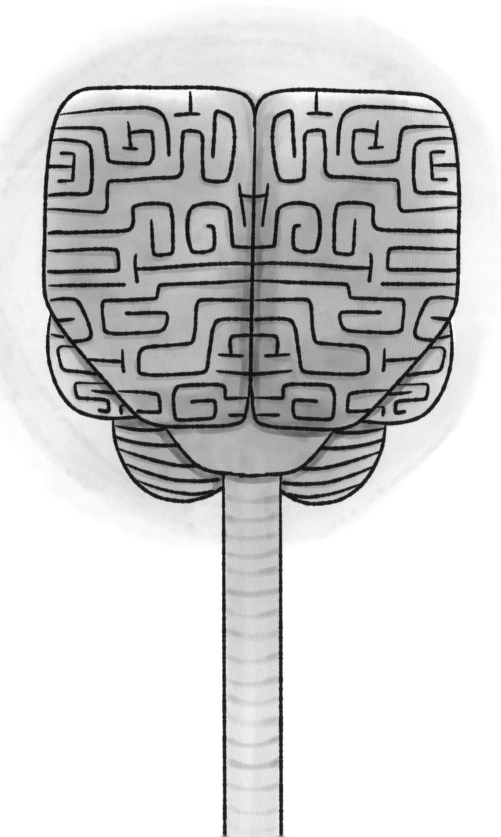

Within the brain there are three parts.
They function together, but also apart.

Dino, instinct defender

Bear Awareness, wise observer

Hippo, memory protector

Dino yells and screams, blaming Hippo for remembering and dreaming...

Hippo responds by pointing at Dino for reacting and screaming.

"Before we blame and bring more shame,"
Bear Awareness Brain exclaims,
"Let's do our ALOHA breath, staying calm and chill,
allowing feelings and thoughts to still."

" Ah, Mouth does what Mouth does; it tastes, it chews.
Feet do what Feet do; they balance, they move.
Hands do what Hands do; they feel, they grab.
Eyes do what Eyes do; they look, they see.
Ears do what Ears do; they listen, they hear.
Nose does what Nose does; it smells.
Lungs do what Lungs do; they contract and expand.
Heart does what Heart does; it beats.
What is it that you do, dear Stomach?"
Bear Awareness calmly asks.

"I digest," Stomach realizes.
  "That's what I do best!"

"And Mouth's doing
    what it does best,
      it tastes and chews!
And Hands are doing
    what they do best,
      they feel, they grab!
And Ears are doing
    what they do best,
      they listen, they hear!"

Bear Awareness smiles,
"Shall we try again what I do best? Aloha Breath!"

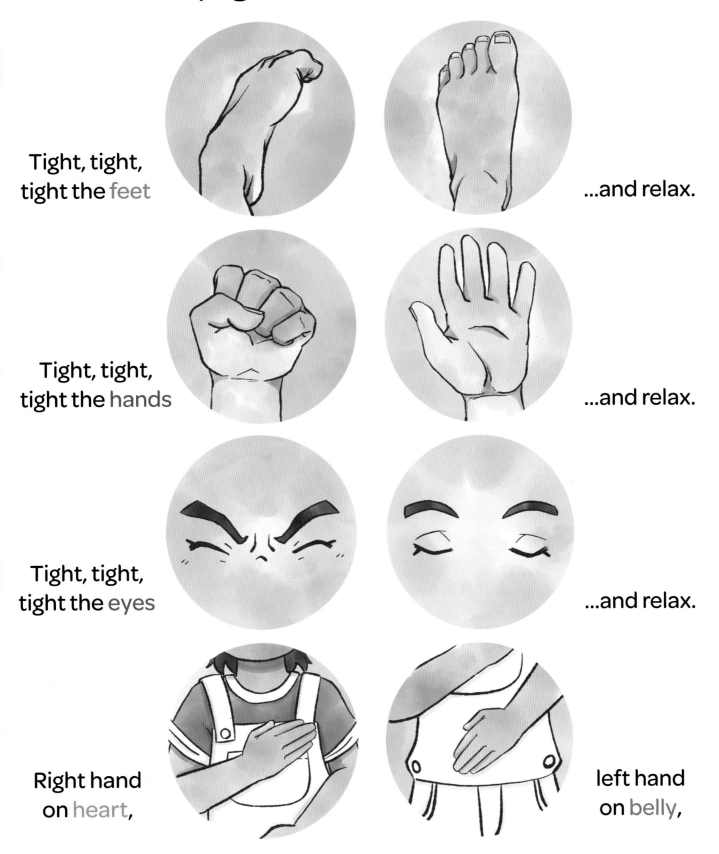

Tight, tight, tight the feet

...and relax.

Tight, tight, tight the hands

...and relax.

Tight, tight, tight the eyes

...and relax.

Right hand on heart,

left hand on belly,

feeling the sensation of breathing.

AKAHAI

Breathe in kindness,
breathe out kindness.

LŌKAHI

Breathe in harmony,
breathe out harmony.

ʻOLUʻOLU

Breathe in gentleness,
breathe out gentleness.

HAʻAHAʻA

Breathe in humility,
breathe out humility.

AHONUI

Breathe in patience,
breathe out patience.

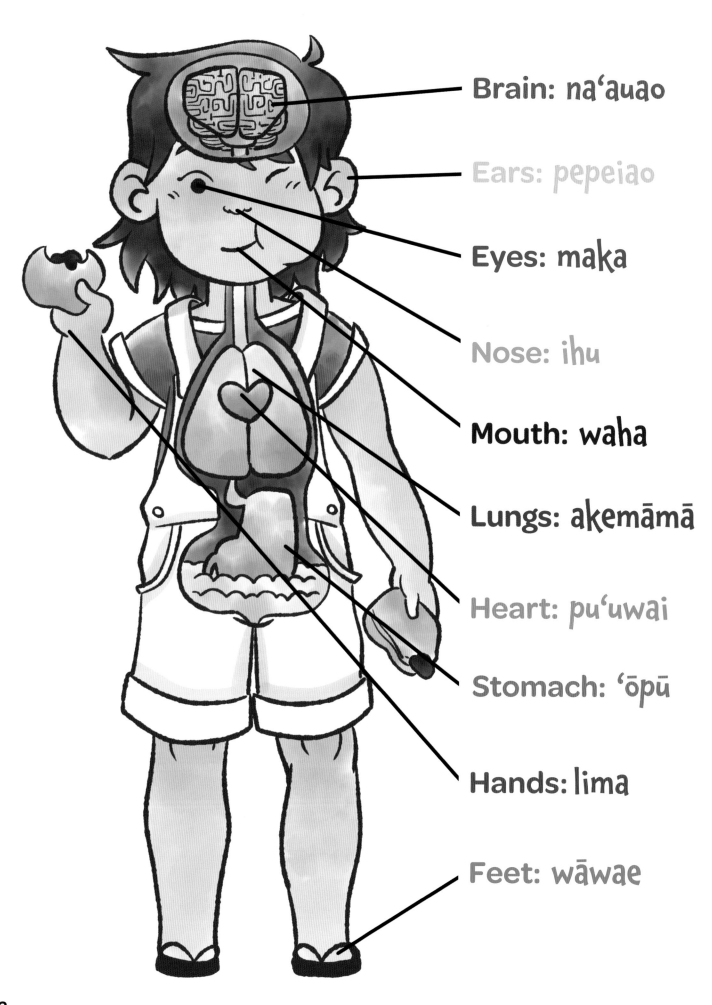

Brain: na'auao

Ears: pepeiao

Eyes: maka

Nose: ihu

Mouth: waha

Lungs: akemāmā

Heart: pu'uwai

Stomach: 'ōpū

Hands: lima

Feet: wāwae

Ke Kino

We are the Body!

Aloha Breath

ALOHA Breath is based on Aunty Pilahi Paki's meaning of aloha as designated in the "Aloha Spirit Law" (HRS [§5-7.5]). It refers to the cultivation of certain attitudes in mind and heart that allows us to connect wholesomely with ourselves and others. Bear Awareness invites us to remember and cultivate each ALOHA value with every in-and-out breath.

Akahai	Kindness	Extending care and love by opening one's heart in full acceptance and embrace.
Lōkahi	Unity	Promoting harmony by recognizing the common humanity and interconnection between all other beings, nature, places and things.
ʻOluʻolu	Gentleness	Speaking and acting with pleasantness and agreeableness.
Haʻahaʻa	Humility	Recognizing that one is not better than any other by acknowledging that one's knowledge, talents, skills are limited.
Ahonui	Patience	Waiting with persistence without expectations of any certain outcome.

and the Brain

Bear Awareness is a play on the term "bare awareness," by Ajahn Brahm, describing our still, observing nature. It refers to the frontal cortex. The frontal cortex is associated with self-regulation, including the ability to practice restraint and wise inquiry.

Hippo refers to the hippocampus, which is part of the mammalian function (limbic system) of the brain. It plays a vital role in storing memories that are strongly associated with emotions and feelings.

Dino refers to the reptilian part, the ancient regulatory function of the brain (heart rate, body temperature, respiration, etc.). It pairs with the limbic system (emotional region) to create emotional states/responses (fight, flight, freeze).

About the Author

Thao "Kale'a" Le, PhD, MPH, is a professor in the Human Development and Family Studies program in the Family Consumer Sciences Department at the University of Hawai'i Mānoa. This is her first children's picture book, an expression of her love and gratitude for Hawai'i.

For audio recordings and more resources,
please visit www.mindfulaloha.org

About the Illustrator

Born and raised on O'ahu, Storm Kano is a recent graduate of the Kapi'olani Community College New Media Arts Program. Rising rapidly in the local art community, she had the recent honor of working on an exhibit for the Japanese American National Museum. Storm's contribution to this book is her way of giving back to the Island community she calls home.

This book made possible with support from

Office of Youth Service